Illustrated by Jeff McGrath

Mauswara
Fish

by Cheri Floyd

Copyright © 2000 by Wesleyan Publishing House
All Rights Reserved
Published by Wesleyan Publishing House
Indianapolis, Indiana 46250
Printed in the United States of America
ISBN 0-89827-209-2

In the Bible, the book of Ecclesiastes says there is a time to talk and a time to keep your mouth shut. I'd like to tell you a story told to me by a wise old man, Pastor Yago, in Papua New Guinea. Listen carefully to find out who knew when to open or shut their mouth and who did not know.

In the Southern Highlands Province of Papua New Guinea there was a pond. And in that pond lived two ducks and a fish. The two ducks swam around, drinking water and eating weeds.

The fish was named Mauswara fish. In Pidgin, the language spoken in Papua New Guinea, "mauswara" means someone who talks too much. And that's exactly what Mauswara fish did.

He talked all the time to his friends the ducks. Many times he bragged about how well he could swim. Mauswara fish also complained to the ducks about rocks on the bottom of the pond and anything else he didn't like. Only once in a while did he tell them nice things, like what great friends they were. Talk, talk, talk. That's all Mauswara fish did.

Even though the ducks were friends with Mauswara fish, sometimes they got tired of hearing him talk. Then they would swim to the edge of the pond and go walking in the grass, catching bugs and enjoying some peace and quiet.

One year a drought came to Papua New Guinea. No rain fell for a long, long time. The grass turned brown. The pond started to dry up. Every day there was less and less water. Soon the ducks and Mauswara fish barely had room to swim.

Mauswara fish complained a lot about the drought. "Why is it so dry? The water is getting muddy. It's hot and I don't like it."

But the ducks didn't complain; they made a plan. They would fly a long way and try to find a new pond with lots of water.

They made Mauswara fish promise to be quiet while they were gone. They said, "You talk so much that the men living in the nearby village will hear you.

"They will come and now that the water is shallow, the men will catch you easily. All they will have to do is scoop you up. You must keep quiet while we are gone."

So the ducks flew away. They traveled a long way, all the way from the far end of the Southern Highlands into the Western Highlands province. And there at last, they found water. Lots and lots of clean water. They quickly flew home to tell Mauswara fish.

As soon as Mauswara fish saw the ducks land, he started talking. "Where have you been and why did you take so long? What did you see?" The ducks said they had found a new home for all three of them and they would take Mauswara fish there.

"Mauswara fish, you get so much practice talking that your jaws must be very strong. We will use a branch and each hold one end in our mouth. You must bite the middle of the branch and hang on. Then we will fly, carrying you with us. Now please keep quiet! The men might hear you talking and come to catch you before we can fly away."

Quickly the ducks found a branch. Mauswara fish bit it and they took off. Up, up, up they went until they were very high in the sky. They were heading toward their new home. As they flew through the air, they passed over the nearby village where the men lived. The men looked up and what a strange thing they saw. Two ducks carrying a fish on a stick! The men were excited and began to shout and point.

Even though he was way up in the air, Mauswara fish heard the men. He felt so proud to have outwitted them. He wanted to tell them what a clever fish he was. He opened his mouth to speak and . . . guess what happened?

That's right. When he opened his mouth to talk, he lost his hold on the branch and fell from the sky.

He fell down, down, down, all the way to the ground and went splat!! And that was the end of Mauswara fish.

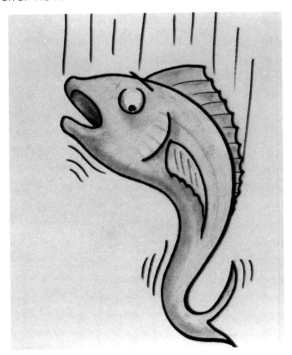

Who knew the right times to open and shut their mouths? That's right, the ducks knew.

Who had no idea when to keep quiet? You guessed it, Mauswara fish. And not knowing when to keep quiet got him into trouble.

God tells us in Proverbs 16:24 that "Pleasant words are a honeycomb, sweet to the soul."

Think about nice words that you can open your mouth to say. You can say thank you when someone gives you a gift. You can also use nice words by giving your mother a compliment or telling your father that you love him. And one of the nicest reasons that you can open your mouth is to tell your friends that Jesus loves them.

The Bible also says in Psalm 34:13, "Keep your tongue from evil and your lips from speaking lies."

We should never tell lies or say bad things. That's the time to keep our mouths shut.

So the next time you are thinking about something, be smart like the ducks. Think about whether it is a good thing to say. If it is, then open your mouth and say it. But if what you are thinking is a way to show off, hurt someone, or sound nasty, then it's the time to close your mouth. Remember this story about Mauswara fish. You don't want to open your mouth at the wrong time.